GREGORY GRIGGS
AND OTHER
NURSERY RHYME PEOPLE

GREGORY GRIGGS

AND OTHER NURSERY RHYME PEOPLE

SELECTED & ILLUSTRATED BY ARNOLD LOBEL

GREENWILLOW BOOKS · A DIVISION OF WILLIAM MORROW & COMPANY, INC., NEW YORK

Library of Congress Cataloging in Publication Data   Lobel, Arnold. Gregory Griggs and other nursery rhyme people.   Summary: A collection of thirty-four nursery rhymes about lesser-known but colorful ladies and gentlemen.   1. Nursery rhymes. [1.   Nursery rhymes]   I.   Title.   PZ8.3.L82Gr   [398.8]   77-22209   ISBN 0-688-80128-5   ISBN 0-688-84128-7 lib. bdg.

TO ADA, AVA AND SUSAN

TABLE OF CONTENTS

Gregory Griggs, Gregory Griggs,
Had twenty-seven different wigs.
He wore them up, he wore them down,
To please the people of the town.
He wore them east, he wore them west,
And never could tell which one he liked best.

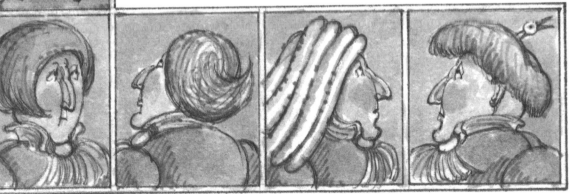

Little Miss Lily,
You're dreadfully silly
To wear such a very long skirt.
If you take my advice,
You would hold it up nice,
And not let it trail in the dirt.

Peter White will ne'er go right.
Would you know the reason why?
He follows his nose wherever he goes,
And that stands all awry.

Charley, Charley,
Stole the barley
Out of the baker's shop.
The baker came out
And gave him a clout,
Which made poor Charley hop.

There was an old man named Michael Finnegan,
He grew a long beard right on his chinnigan,
Along came a wind and blew it in again...
Poor old Michael Finnegan.

Jerry Hall
He is so small,
A rat could eat him,
Hat and all.

The giant Jim, great giant grim,
Wears a hat without a brim,
Weighs a ton, and wears a blouse,
And trembles when he meets a mouse.

15

There was an old woman tossed up in a basket
Nineteen times as high as the moon;
Where she was going I couldn't but ask it,
For in her hand she carried a broom.

"Old Woman, old woman, old woman," said I,
"O whither, O whither, O whither, so high?"
"To brush the cobwebs off the sky!
And I'll be back again by and by."

Little Miss Tuckett
Sat on a bucket,
Eating some peaches and cream.
There came a grasshopper
And tried hard to stop her,
But she said, "Go away, or I'll scream."

Theophilus Thistle, the successful thistle sifter,
When sifting a sieve full of unsifted thistles,
Thrust three thousand thistles through the thick of his thumb.
If Theophilus Thistle, the successful thistle sifter,
Can thrust three thousand thistles through the thick of his thumb,
Take care, when sifting a sieve full of unsifted thistles,
Thrust not three thousand thistles through the thick of thy thumb.

Little Clotilda, well and hearty,
Thought she'd like to give a party.
But her friends were shy and wary.
Nobody came but her own canary.

Punch and Judy
Fought for a pie,
Punch gave Judy
A sad blow in the eye.

Says Punch to Judy,
"Will you have more?"
Says Judy to Punch,
"My eye is sore."

Dingty diddledy, my mammy's maid,
She stole oranges, I am afraid—
Some in her pocket, some in her sleeve—
She stole oranges, I do believe.

Terence McDiddler,
The three-stringed fiddler,
Can charm, if you please,
The fish from the seas.

Little Tee Wee,

He went to sea,

In an open boat.

And while afloat

The little boat bended

And my story's ended.

Milkman, milkman, where have you been?
In buttermilk channel up to my chin.
I spilt my milk and I spoilt my clothes,
And got a long icicle hung to my nose.

There was a fat man of Bombay,
Who was smoking one sunshiny day,
When a bird called a snipe flew away with his pipe,
Which vexed the fat man of Bombay.

The greedy man is he who sits
And bites bits out of plates,
Or else takes up an almanac
And gobbles all the dates.

27

This little man lived all alone,
And he was a man of sorrow;
For, if the weather was fair today,
He was sure it would rain tomorrow.

There was a maid on Scrabble Hill,
And if not dead, she lives there still.
She grew so tall, she reached the sky,
And on the moon, hung clothes to dry.

Hark, hark, the dogs do bark,
The beggars are coming to town;
Some in jags, and some in rags,
And some in velvet gowns.

Some gave them white bread,
And some gave them brown,
And some gave them a good horse-whip,
And sent them out of town.

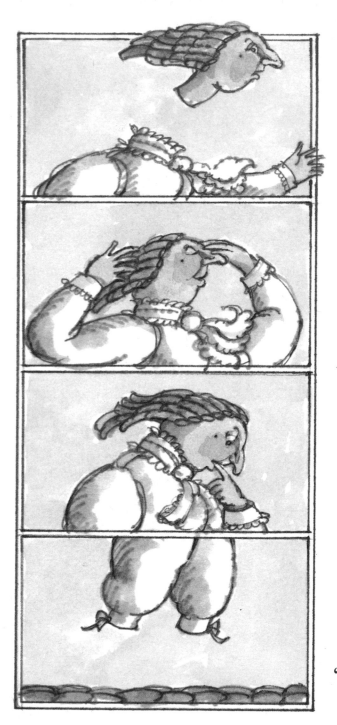

As I was going out one day,
My head fell off and rolled away.

But when I saw that it was gone,
I picked it up and put it on.

And when I went into the street,
A fellow cried, "Look at your feet!"

I looked at them and sadly said,
"I've left them both asleep in bed!"

Handy-spandy,
Jack-a-Dandy,
Loves plum cake
and sugar candy.
He bought some
at a grocer's shop,
And out he came,
hop, hop, hop, hop.

One day a boy went walking
And walked into a store.
He bought a pound of sausage meat,
And laid it on the floor.
The boy began to whistle—
He whistled up a tune,
And all the little sausages
Danced around the room.

Hannah Bantry,
In the pantry,
Gnawing at a mutton bone;
How she gnawed it,
How she clawed it,
When she found herself alone.

"I know I have lost my train,"
  Said a man named Joshua Lane;
"But I'll run on the rails
  With my coat-tails for sails
  And maybe I'll catch it again."

There was a mad man,
And he had a mad wife,
And they lived all in a mad lane!
They had three children all at a birth,
And they too were mad every one.
The father was mad,
The mother was mad,
The children all mad beside;
And upon a mad horse they all of them got,
And madly away did ride.

37

Anna Elise
She jumped with surprise;
The surprise was so quick,
It played her a trick;
The trick was so rare,
She jumped in a chair;
The chair was so frail,
She jumped in a pail;
The pail was so wet,
She jumped in a net;
The net was so small,
She jumped on a ball;
The ball was so round,
She jumped on the ground;
And ever since then
She's been turning around.

Nose, nose, jolly red nose,
And what gave you that jolly red nose?
Nutmegs and cinnamon, spices and cloves,
And they gave me this jolly red nose.

Who are you?
A dirty old man.
I've always been
since the day I began,
Mother and Father
were dirty before me,
Hot or cold water
has never come o'er me.

In a cottage in Fife
Lived a man and his wife,
Who, believe me, were comical folk;
For, to people's surprise,
They both saw with their eyes,
And their tongues moved whenever they spoke!
When quite fast asleep,
I've been told that to keep
Their eyes open they could not contrive;
They walked on their feet,
And 'twas thought what they eat
Helped, with drinking, to keep them alive!
What's amazing to tell,
I have heard that their smell
Chiefly lay in a thing call'd their nose!
And though strange are such tales,
On their fingers they'd nails,
As well as on each of their toes!

Alas! alas! for Miss Mackay!
Her knives and forks have run away;
And when the cups and spoons are going,
She's sure there is no way of knowing.

There was a young farmer of Leeds,
Who swallowed six packets of seeds.
It soon came to pass
He was covered with grass,
And he couldn't sit down for the weeds.

Flying-man, Flying-man,
Up in the sky,
Where are you going to,
Flying so high?

Over the mountains
And over the sea,
Flying-man, Flying-man
Can't you take me?

AFTERWORD

As I began to think about this collection of nursery rhymes, the task of selection seemed overwhelming. I realized that I had to choose from several centuries of accumulated treasure. Early in my research I saw that within the nursery rhyme literature—that noisy, milling throng of dogs and cats and pigs and clowns—there existed an exuberant and courageous race of human beings. In a nonsensical way they seem to mirror all of our own struggles with the rigors of contemporary living. I decided to focus the attention of my book on these ladies and gentlemen.

Humpty Dumpty and Old King Cole are not to be found here. Like pictures that have hung on the wall in the same places for too long, they have more or less disappeared for me. It was the lesser-known faces that jumped out, made me want to draw them: Hannah Bantry, turning her dark pantry into a battle ground of conflicting guilt and greed; Terence McDiddler, taking his fiddle down to the sea to become an Orpheus reborn; the maid from Scrabble Hill, cleverly fitting her alarming deformity to fine washday advantage. And of course, the relentlessly indecisive Gregory Griggs, working his way toward a new attitude of relaxed baldness.

Bringing this parade of Mother Goose people to these pages gave me great pleasure. I hope that you have enjoyed them as well.

A.L. 1978